Laura and the Bandits

Alice and Emil's grandparents come to stay and the family decide to take a picnic on the beach. Sniffing around the cliffs, Laura makes a strange discovery and before long the whole family is involved in a very exciting plot.

For Granny and Pompey.

Philippe Dumas

Laura
and the Bandits

FONTANA · LIONS

First published in France 1978 by L'Ecole
des Loisirs
First published in Great Britain 1980 by
Victor Gollancz Ltd
First published in Fontana Lions June 1982
by William Collins Sons & Co Ltd
14 St James's Place, London SW1

© 1978 L'Ecole des Loisirs, Paris

Printed in Great Britain by
Richard Clay (The Chaucer Press) Ltd,
Bungay, Suffolk

Granny and Grandad
had just arrived from England
to spend a holiday with
their French grandchildren.

They brought some English sweets
(forbidden by the dentist)
and an enormous bone
(forbidden by the Customs)

which made everybody
very happy.

The next morning was so lovely
that they decided to take a
picnic to the beach.

Mum cut the bread,
Dad made the sandwiches,

Alice washed some fruit
and Emil found the thermos flask.

Grandad boiled some eggs.

Granny packed everything
into a basket.

At last everyone was ready.

As usual, Laura had
the best seat in the car.

They turned off the main road
and went along a narrow track.

There is a gap in the cliffs.

Hardly anyone knows about it.

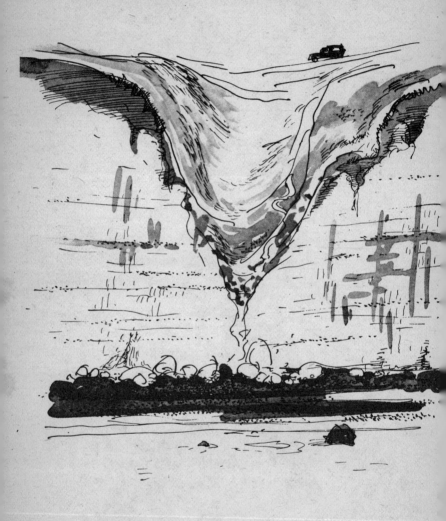

It's like the end of the world.

They had to earn their lunch
with a bit of exercise.

They made a fire with wood that

the sea had thrown on to the beach.

And, since they were on a
beach, they had a swim.

Laura looked after the children.

Then everyone got dry and warmed themselves in front of the fire.

Now they were ready for lunch.

Laura wandered about,
sniffing here and there
and chasing seagulls.

Suddenly she began to bark.

"It's as if she wants us to follow her."

Alice and Emil went with Laura.

She led them to
a gap in the cliff.
They went straight in.

Just inside they found a
rubber dinghy. It seemed
a funny place for it to be.

"Let's go and get the grown-ups."

Dad and Grandad came this time
and they all set off down a dark tunnel.

It was rather frightening.

They came to a big room with
concrete walls. Grandad said it must
have been built in the war.

Emil found a light switch
and turned on the light.

There was a table with some food
on it which didn't look as though it
had been there very long.

They discovered a sort of dormitory
and in another room a huge pile of
tinned food – enough for an army.
There was a locked door as well.
But Laura took care of that.

They found a room stuffed with
treasure including a famous
painting which they knew had
been stolen from the Louvre
some months before.

"What a find!"

Then Laura sensed something.

Quickly they switched off the light
as they heard footsteps approaching.

Three men came in, talking loudly.
They seemed quite at home and
looked very menacing.

They were robbers and they
carried revolvers! They put
their guns on the table while
they drank some wine.

It seemed from what they said
that a boat was coming that
evening to take the valuable
painting away so that it could be sold.
The bandits had to be stopped.

Once again Laura took charge.
With a low growl . . .

. . . she sprang at the men.
They were so taken by surprise,
that Dad managed to seize their guns.

They tied up the bandits and
everyone was given their orders.
Emil was sent to tell Mum and
Granny what they had found.
Grandad went to fetch the police.
Alice, Dad and, of course, Laura
stayed behind to guard the villains.

Granny and Mum had begun to
get worried. Then Emil arrived,
told them what had happened,
and warned them that the boat might
arrive at any minute.

Meanwhile, Grandad roared off on
a motor bike, borrowed from the
bandits.

At the police station, the
policeman finally decided
that there might be something
to the elderly Englishman's story.

Very quietly, the police surrounded
the entrance to the cave.

When it got dark more bandits
landed on the beach.

When they were all inside the cave
the police moved in.

It was chaotic.

Alice and Dad kept the
newcomers at bay.

Laura captured their boss.

It was soon over. They were
handcuffed together.

A man from the museum arrived by
helicopter to recover his precious
painting. Some journalists had
come with him. The insurance company
gave the family a big reward for finding
the picture.

There was enough to build a sports centre

and a library for the village children.

On the day of the grand opening
the Mayor made a splendid speech
in which he thanked Laura and
awarded her a special key to the
building.